KU-711-596

Picture Kelpies is an imprint of Floris Books. First published in 2013 by Floris Books. Fifth printing 2016
Text © 2013 Chani McBain Illustrations © 2013 Kirsteen Harris-Jones. Chani McBain and Kirsteen Harris-Jones
assert their right under the Copyright, Designs and Patents Act 1988 to be recognised as the Author and
Illustrator of this Work. All rights reserved. No part of this book may be reproduced without prior permission of
Floris Books, Edinburgh www.florisbooks.co.uk
The publisher acknowledges subsidy from Creative Scotland towards the publication of this volume.
British Library CIP Data available ISBN 978-086315-953-4 Printed in China through Asia Pacific Offset Ltd

For Mum and Garvie (fellow Nessie-hunters) and Niamh (a great audience). CMB

To TJ and Rosie — Never give up! KHJ

No Such Thing as NESSIE

CHANI McBAIN and KIRSTEEN HARRIS-JONES

Finlay loved dinosaurs.

He loved triceratops and stegosaurus and tyrannosaurus rex,
but his favourite dinosaur was the

Loch Ness Monster.

Finlay's gran said she had once seen Nessie. A big head had popped out from the water of Loch Ness and watched his gran eating her lunch, back when she was a little girl.

Finlay's gran hadn't been surprised, because she'd always believed in the Loch Ness Monster. She'd thrown Nessie some shortbread. Nessie had chomped it all up and then ...

splash!
she was gone.

Now Finlay was going on holiday to Gran's house and he was planning his very own Nessie hunt.

Mum drove them along the twisty road towards Loch Ness.

Finlay saw a dark shape over the hill. It had two humps just like ...

"Mum! Nessie!" he yelled.

Screeech!

Mum slammed her foot on the brake.
"Finlay, don't shout like that. It's dangerous."
"But Mum, there's Nessie," Finlay pointed ...

"Loch Ness Tractor Repairs," Mum read the sign.

"There's no such thing as Nessie, silly," said Finlay's
big sister, Sarah.
"Don't worry, Finlay. I'm sure Gran will help you
with your Nessie hunt," said Mum.

When Finlay arrived at Gran's house she agreed they could start looking for Nessie right away.

Finlay packed his Nessie-hunting kit, which had his camera, pencils, a notepad and a net in it, and he wrapped up some of Gran's shortbread too, just in case.

They all went for a walk along a pebbly beach.
Finlay skipped a stone across the loch.

ssssSSSSSSsss

"What's that noise, Gran?"

It was coming from a big pile of
rocks down the beach.
Sticking out from behind the biggest rock was
a strange shape. It looked a bit like a tail!

"Gran! Nessie!"

Finlay shouted and ran towards the tail ...

But this Nessie was rather floppy.

sssSSSSSSSss

SSSSSSSSSS

"Sorry, Finlay" said Gran. "It looks like someone's forgotten their blow-up Nessie.
It must have a hole somewhere."
"There's no such thing as Nessie," said Sarah, sticking her tongue out.

The next day, Gran took Finlay and Sarah on a boat trip.
Finlay stood right at the front holding on tight to the rail.
All the passengers were distracted by an osprey swooping down,
hitting the water with a big splash and flapping off with a fish.

Rising a bit further away was a grey shape with a long, grey neck.

"Everyone! It's Nessie!" shouted Finlay.

They all rushed to see ...

The long, grey neck slowly lifted out of the water. Its body was dark and shiny and ...

square?

"Sorry folks," shouted the boat skipper. "That's one of the research submarines doing her rounds."

"*Awwwww!*" The tourists groaned.

"Told you there's no such thing as Nessie," Sarah said, again.

The skipper gave Finlay's shoulder a squeeze. "Better luck next time, eh, son?"

The next day Finlay, Sarah and Gran were exploring the woods near the loch. They heard leaves rustling.

"Well I don't think that's Nessie," his gran smiled. "Let's find out what it is."

They tiptoed through the trees towards the edge of the loch and keeked out from behind a tree. A beautiful stag was having a drink.

As they watched the stag, Finlay noticed a long, dark shape on the water, getting larger and closer. It was huge.

He started to feel a bit nervous.
What if Nessie wasn't friendly after all?

"Ggggran… Nnnnessie…" he stuttered.

A red crane rolled out from the trees, casting its long shadow across the water.

The stag leapt away, back into the woods.

"There's no such thing as..."

"Shh, now, Sarah," said Gran. She gave Finlay's hand a squeeze.

Finlay sighed. "Can we go home now, Gran?"

On the last day of their holiday, Sarah went shopping with Mum, while Finlay and Gran visited Urquhart Castle and then headed off for a picnic.

Finlay put his hands deep in his pockets and walked around kicking the grass.

"What's wrong, Finlay?" his gran asked.

"There's **no such thing** as Nessie."

His gran looked at him. "Ach, Finlay,
I bet she's just shy."

Finlay picked up a big chunk of shortbread and chucked it as hard
as he could into the loch behind him. It made a big plop.

"Nessie doesn't exist!" he yelled.

Crunch,
crunch,
crunch...

"Finlay! Nessie!" Gran shouted.

He whirled around. A big head and a long thick neck rose out of the bubbling loch. She had little black eyes and a wide face, and she was chewing.

Finlay stared at the Loch Ness Monster. Nessie stared back.

Quick! His camera! He had to get his camera! He turned round, grabbed his bag, turned back –

But Nessie was gone.

Finlay started to laugh and Gran joined in.

"I don't care that I don't have a picture!" Finlay exclaimed.

"I saw Nessie, Gran!

I saw the Loch Ness
Monster."

His gran laughed so hard that she could hardly talk.
"And she still likes my shortbread."

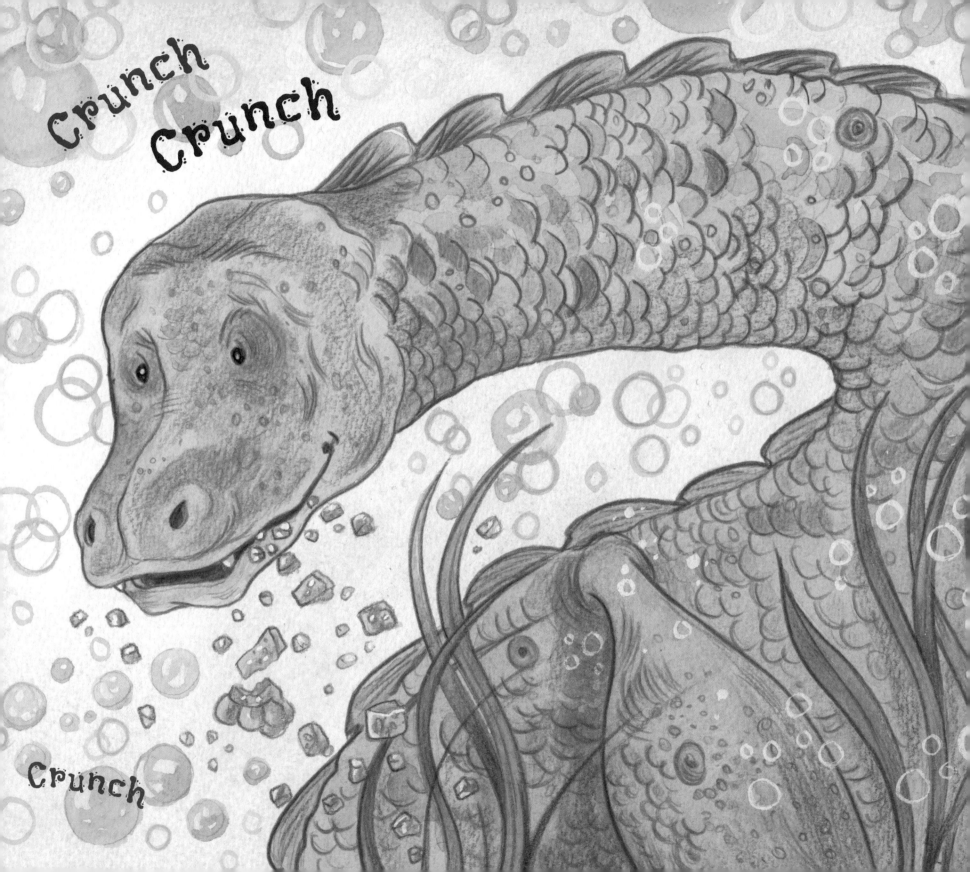